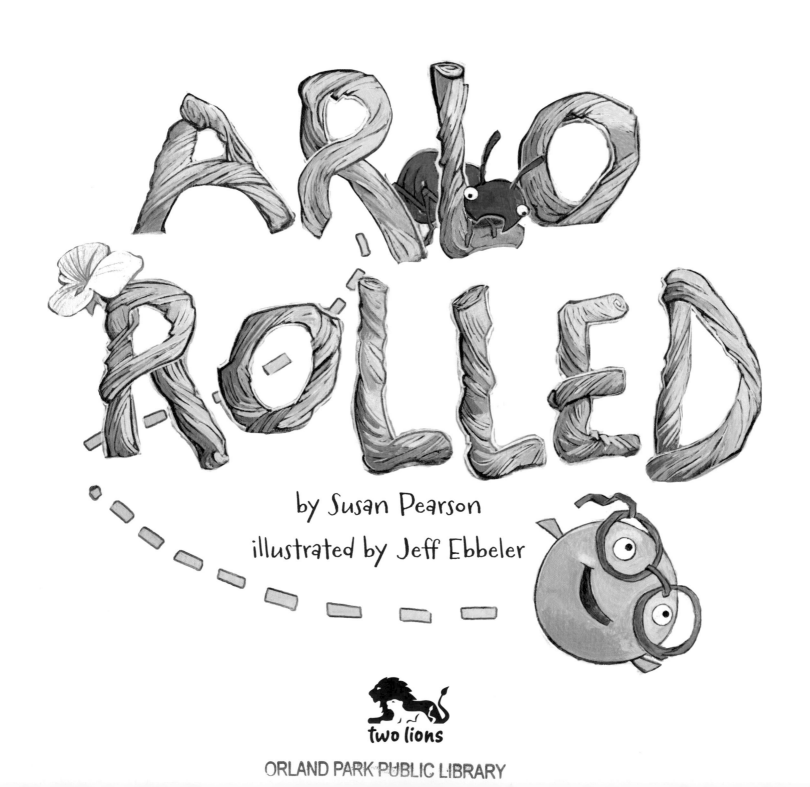

ARLO ROLLED

by Susan Pearson

illustrated by Jeff Ebbeler

two lions

two lions

Amazon Publishing
Attn: Amazon Children's Publishing
P.O. Box 400818
Las Vegas, NV 89140
www.amazon.com/amazonchildrenspublishing

Library of Congress Cataloging-in-Publication Data is available upon request.

ISBN-13: 9781477847213 (hardcover)
ISBN-10: 1477847219 (hardcover)
ISBN-13: 9781477897218 (eBook)
ISBN-10: 1477897216 (eBook)

The illustrations are rendered in acrylic paint on paper.

Book design by JenDraws
Editor: Margery Cuyler

Printed in China (R)
First edition
10 9 8 7 6 5 4 3 2 1

To gardeners everywhere—S.P.

To my dad, who inspired
my love of gardening—J.E.

At the end of the garden,
next to the berries,

lived Mary and Gary and Terry and Sherry . . .

and Arlo—

five peas in a pod—
a plump, fat, green group,
perfect for salads
and stir-fries and soup.

"NO WAY!"
said Arlo.

"Stir-fries and soup
are no life for me!
I want to grow up
and find out what I'll be."

So he dropped to the ground
with the tiniest sound . . .

until he bumped into
a hungry gray slug.
"Stay for awhile," said the slug,
"if you please.
Ask anyone here—I adore peas!"

and he rolled off before the slug could reply.
"Being lunch for a slug is no life for me!

I want to grow up and find out what I'll be."

He rolled through some poppies and lamb's ears and pinks,

but what was that smell? Arlo wondered, What stinks?

Then two nasty pincers reached out to stab him— a stink bug was just about ready to grab him.

What a disaster! Arlo rolled faster!

Past iris and peonies
Arlo rolled on . . .

right out of the garden and onto the lawn.
A pea on a spree in the spring.
What a fling!

"What have we here?" said a deep voice. "Hello! No one admires a pea like a crow!"

Oh, no! thought Arlo. I have a hunch that old Mr. Crow would like me for lunch!

Arlo did not wait around for a minute. A crow was nice ONLY if he wasn't in it.

Then an army of ants came along in a line.

"SNACK ATTACK!"

"SNACK ATTACK!" they all said with a whine.

But Arlo was bigger and bolder—and fast.
He rolled right on past.

Ahead was a puppy digging a hole,
frantically trying to capture a mole.

Puppy dug. Hole grew. Pebbles sprayed. Dirt blew.

Puppy kicked. Arlo FLEW!

He sailed to a field where he dropped with a PLOP, rolled into a wall, and came to a stop.

"I want to grow up
and find out what I'll be,
but right now I'm pooped!"
said Arlo, and he . . .

fell fast asleep.

Arlo slept . . .

and slept . . .

and slept.

Who knew
that while he slept,
Arlo GREW!

Until one sunny spring day, Arlo woke up.

He stretched

and he strrrrretched

toward the sun—it felt fine!

"NOW WATCH ME!" he shouted
and started to twine
up the wall. "I'M A VINE!"

Arlo was so happy, he blossomed.

The sun shone warm,
the breezes blew.
Arlo grew . . . and grew . . .
and grew.

His blossoms fell,
but in their places,
dangling from the
empty spaces

were PEAPODS!

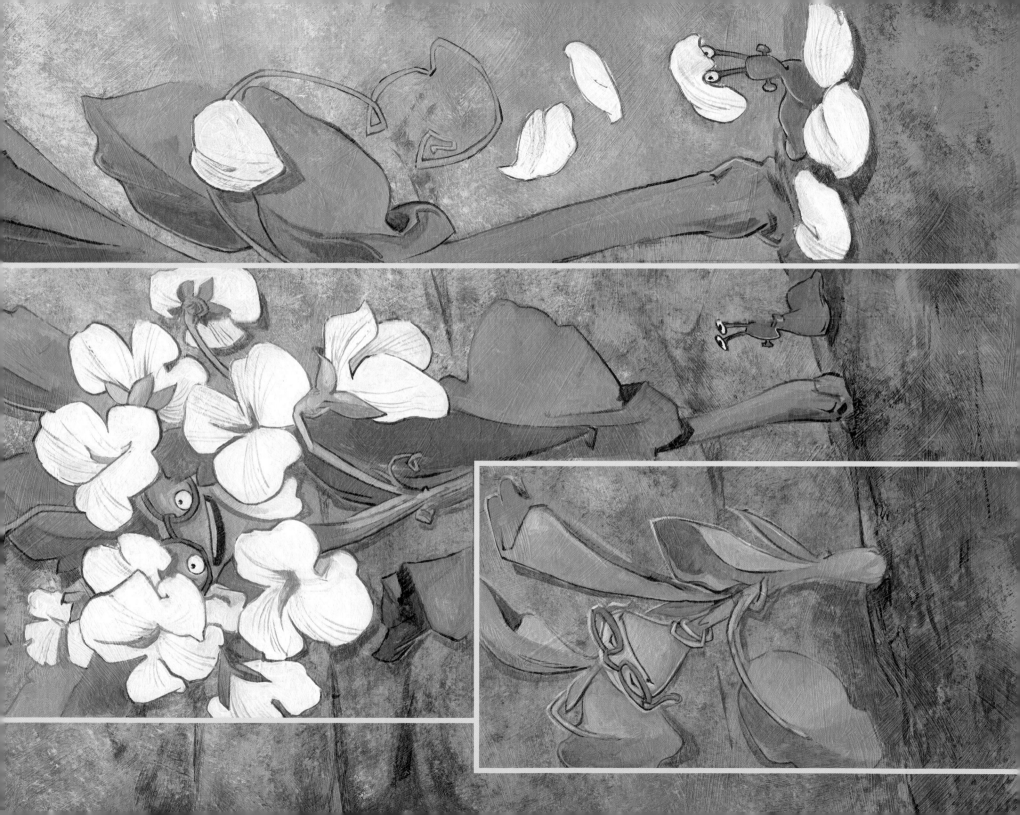

Now over the field, right next to the wall live Molly and Holly and Dolly and Paul . . . and Arlene!